Scholars to the

"Book 2 was amazing witł where Maggie and James f .... their new school. Overall my favourite bit is where the scholars had to battle it out in the New Forest. I recommend it for ages 7-10, I really look forward to reading book 3" **Oscar age 8.**

"I really liked Storm, she reminded me of my dogs. I like how she's cute and confident and how they have a telepathic connection. I liked that Vince came back in this story and how he is confident all the time. I am excited for book 3 and I really hope they go to a new realm to explore" **Griff age 10.**

"I love this book because it is exciting and adventurous. My favourite character is Storm because she is funny when she jumps up and talks. My favourite scene is when they try to catch The Snatcher because there were all sorts of problems.I like pictures in the books because it shows more detail and lets you use your imagination. In the next book I would like to know what Maggie's plan is. I would also like to find out what Storm does in the next book!" **Emi, age 7**

Titles in the Below the Green series

Book 1 - Underground Adventure

Book 2 - Scholars to the Rescue

Book 3 - Battle for the Enchanted Ring

Book 4 - Enchanted Ring Rescue Mission

Book 5 - Victory in the Sky Realm

To order copies of these, please go to getbook. at/UndergroundAdventure to choose from print, audio or ebook. Alternatively contact the author at arhetheringtonbooks@gmail.com

Copyright © 2020 by A. R. Hetherington

SECOND EDITION

www.arhetherington.com

About the Author

The author spent several years in Africa growing up and it is here that she first developed her love of reading due to there being no TV or other technology.

Her dad would tell her and her sister stories every week on their way back from their weekly visit to the library a couple of hours away. They were unique and creative stories which they both absolutely loved.

She has had all sorts of jobs over the years including horticulture, design and translation. For several years now she has been teaching primary school children part time as well as writing her fantasy adventures.

The author lives in a tiny rural village with her husband, lots of fancy hens and two mad spaniels called Rosie and Mabel. Her own boy and girl are grown up now and off creating adventures of their own.

For more information please visit her website at www.arhetherington.com

AR Hetherington

This book is for my readers, thank you for sharing the adventure!

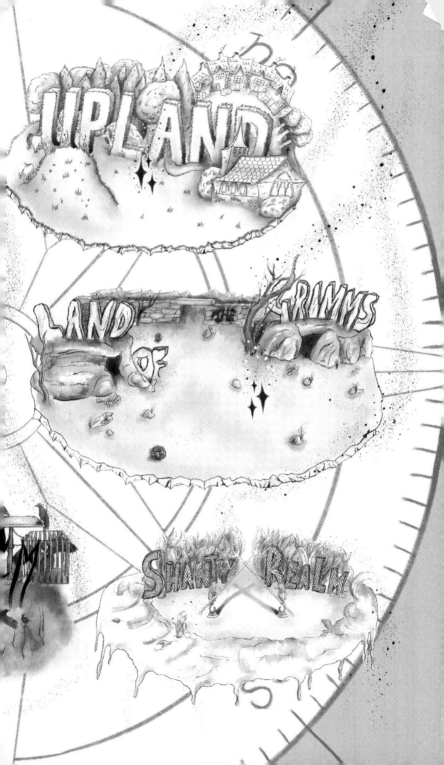

Contents

CHAPTER 1

The First Day of School

"You are the cutest dog ever!" Maggie tickled Storm's tummy as the puppy lay on the grass, paws in the air, with a look of contentment and pride on her face.

"I can't help being adorable," Storm replied and leaned up to nuzzle Maggie under the chin. Maggie couldn't help but laugh. Storm was a birthday gift when she had turned 8 and they were already the— best of friends. Very few people had a dog that they could not only talk to but could understand too. But then Maggie had a rare connection with animals; a gift which was about to be further developed in The School of Noble Beasts. She was just waiting, a

11

little impatiently, for her friend James to arrive and then they would head off for their first day at school.

Not everyone would be as excited at the thought of the first day back to school, especially as this was an extra school to the normal one she went to, but then this was not an ordinary school nor was it in an ordinary place. Maggie had discovered a portal to a whole new land with many realms below the cricket green in her village. James and Maggie had recently come back from an extraordinary underground adventure and had been invited, by their new Earthlie friends, to join them at school to develop their new and exciting talents. These had been identified recently at an important ceremony in the Earthlie Realm.

"Hurry up James!" Maggie urged, as she saw James ambling along the grass towards her. His head was down and he looked lost in thought as usual.

"Come on, we can't be late for our first day James!" Maggie was jumping up and down with her usual high levels of excitement and energy. Storm pounced on James' shoes as he arrived and he looked up at them in surprise."

"Am I late?"

"No, you're not; I just can't wait to get going. Storm, get off his shoes!"

Storm had taken a shine to James; she always knew when someone had a kind heart. James, however, was a little nervous of Storm, due in part to her bouncy and playful nature; but also as she had a habit of licking his shoes and even his trousers. This did not strike him as hygienic at all.

Meanwhile, Maggie heaved up the crumbly, old trapdoor which lay hidden just below the grass. The expected little shimmer of glittery dust was released, accompanied by a muffled 'whomph'. Maggie led the way, glancing over her shoulder to check that Storm and James were following. She couldn't wait to see Quinn and Vita again. Down the familiar stone steps they went to the welcoming light below.

"Hello!" Maggie called out, as soon as she spotted their new friends. How kind of them to come and meet them at the Glimmer. This was the term the

Earthlies used for a portal.

"Hello! How are you both?" Quinn greeted them, and without waiting for an answer continued, "Who do we have here?" Storm bounded up to them, wagging her tail at such a speed that it was almost a blur.

"This is Storm, my new dog, though perhaps you would call her my 'companion'?" Maggie recalled that the Earthlies did not own pets and considered it quite an honour if an animal or bird chose to befriend you.

Down by his feet Quinn could hear some muffled puppy snuffles.

"Well, aren't you a gorgeous creature?" he said kneeling down to offer his hand for a sniff.

"Storm says hello and that yes she is rather gorgeous, even if she says so herself," Maggie translated for them. "It seems Storm is rather confident!"

Vita laughed. "Hello James, school starts soon and we don't have much time to see the others on our way. Let's get going."

Quinn and Maggie chatted all the way along the

tunnel with Storm bounding around their feet. Vita and James fell into step behind them with Vita chatting animatedly. There was a lot to catch up on, as time had a strange way of slowing down and sometimes even speeding up in the Earthlie realm. It was hard to keep track of how much time had passed each time they visited. Not much as it happened, on this occasion, since their last visit. There was still a sense of excitement after the recent Colour Ceremony revealing which skill set each Scholar had. All four of them were in different schools, so they agreed that they would meet in the main clearing of the forest at lunchtime.

They strolled out from the tunnel and into the glorious morning sunshine. Maggie felt she would never tire of the magnificent forest and glades which were filled with ingenious tree houses where the Earthlies lived.

"Anyone feeling nervous?" Vita asked, "I know I am, a bit."

James nodded but Maggie was feeling excited and she couldn't stop smiling. She had met Wolfe briefly on the night of the Colour Ceremony. The Ancient

Scholar, who was in charge of her school, had steely grey hair with shimmering pearl streaks running through it. Initially he had seemed a little serious and quite intense but she felt sure he would be a fantastic teacher.

"Don't worry, Vita." Quinn tried to encourage his younger sister. "You will all love it and by lunchtime you will wonder why you felt worried at all. I promise."

Quinn was about to enter his second year as a scholar in The School of Magic and Marvel. He could already cleverly manipulate certain things around him and Maggie was keen to see what he would learn next. His skills had certainly helped them all out on their last trip when they had ventured to the Grimms' realm. Maggie shivered as some of the scarier memories flooded back.

Just then the principal scholar, Keithia, with her gorgeous long, white curls streaked with emerald green, strode into the middle of the clearing they had just reached. Everyone hushed instantly and turned to hear what she had to say.

"Welcome scholars," she began, "and a very special

welcome to all you Implings who are leaving your younger play days behind to become true Earthlie scholars. Today is the beginning of a journey like no other. Each of you has a unique role to play in our community and I will be watching your development closely. The Ancients are here with me to welcome you. Follow their instructions carefully, for they are the very best in their field. You will be challenged, you will have to train hard but you will not regret a moment spent in their care."

With that Keithia turned and strode away leaving behind an increasing hubbub of chatter as all the scholars, old and new, made their way over to their Ancient. Most of the Ancients were surrounded by a small crowd, but Maggie and Storm slipped through the others to find Wolfe standing alone beside the most enormous dog they had ever seen. Storm immediately lay down, resting her head on her paws. This was the first time Maggie had seen her do anything remotely humble. She was intrigued by her puppy's reaction to the older dog.

"Hello Maggie," said Wolfe in his low, gentle voice, "allow me to introduce you to my companion

Jedrek. I see you have a new companion with you too." Wolfe's eyes twinkled in amusement as he took in the sight of this sleek, silvery young puppy with her huge paws.

"This is Storm," offered Maggie," she is actually quite a lively and confident character normally." Storm raised an eyebrow at Maggie but stayed low to the ground.

Wolfe chuckled. He had already read Storm's character; he was after all, the Ancient of the School of Noble Beasts.

"She is showing respect to my companion," he explained, "you aren't the only one who will need training. Storm too will be learning how things work in our Realm. Jed will show her the ropes." Jedrek took a step closer to Storm and, leaning forward, grazed the top of Storm's head lightly with her chin. With that, Storm bounded back up and her tail started wagging again at top speed. She did, however, stick close to Maggie's legs as Wolfe led the way deeper into the forest.

"Now, let us begin." Wolfe called back over his shoulder and Maggie's tummy somersaulted.

19

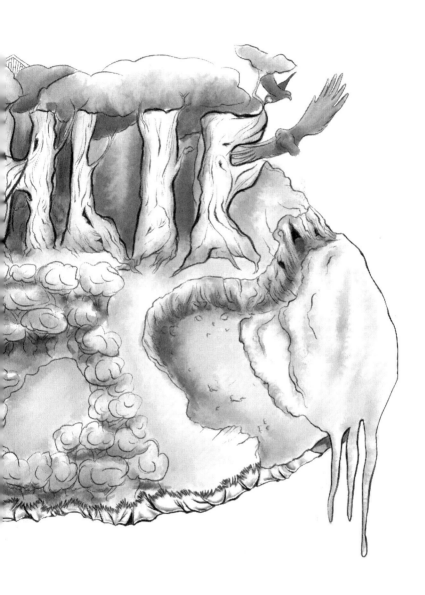

Maggie

Deeper into the forest they strode but Maggie's heart felt light and bright. Sunlight dappled through the canopy and bird song followed them each step of the way. She recognised some of the birds from home, or Upland as the Earthlies would say; blue tits, black birds, a robin and a little wren. Some birds were completely new to her however and she couldn't wait to learn more.

A short while later the forest thinned, revealing a tranquil glade, speckled with wild flowers and gorgeous butterflies flitting between them. Maggie gasped as she caught sight of a log cabin, in front of which was quite an assortment of creatures. There were two deer nestling into each other, a golden pheasant scratching the ground nearby, a red squirrel looking directly at them and a rather large pig sunbathing in a dusty patch. What had really made Maggie catch her breath however, was the goigil standing proudly to one side of the cabin, shaking its stately head and feathery mane. The scales along her regal back rippled and glinted in the sunlight and her wings were tucked neatly to her sides. Maggie glanced up at Wolfe with the question shining from her eyes. She had seen such creatures in the Grimms' realm before. They were magnificent creatures, part horse and part dragon perhaps, something like a Pegasus but the size of a giant Shire horse. The ones she had seen had been captured by the Grimms and enslaved; made to pull waggons to market. They had been miserable and bad tempered. This marvellous creature, however, seemed perfectly at ease and her wonderful grey eyes gazed with interest at Maggie. Her scales were a shimmering grey colour and her showy mane flickered like pale flames of fire.

"This is Selene," introduced Wolfe, "we have managed to free many goigils from the Grimms over the years, but this particular friend insisted on coming home with us."

Maggie edged closer to Selene, who bowed her head to return the greeting, before approaching Maggie on giant hooves. The goigil leaned her strong, graceful neck down low, so that her soft muzzle could tickle Maggie's cheek.

"Welcome, little one, I have been waiting."

"Oh!" was all Maggie could manage in reply. She was completely bowled over by this awesome animal and, on top of that, Selene could also speak to her!

Wolfe watched the brief exchange with a thoughtful look in his eyes.

"Come," he interrupted, "time to meet the others."

Again Maggie looked up in surprise. As Wolfe had met her alone in the clearing she hadn't given any thought yet as to whom else might be there. Keithia had told her at the Colour Ceremony that her gift was extremely rare, so Maggie had been unsure as to how many scholars there might be in the School of Noble Beasts. In fact there were only three people seated on the porch which surrounded the cabin. She hadn't seen them at first as they blended incredibly well into the natural surroundings. A woman, almost as tall as Wolfe, stood up from a gnarled wooden chair. Her hair was closely cropped; silvery grey with the now familiar pearl streaks glinting here and there. Her gaze was direct and enquiring but there was kindness there too.

"This is Britta, my companion." Wolfe smiled warmly as Britta strode over to them. She surprised Maggie by enveloping her in a warm, tight hug.

"I'm so pleased to meet you, Maggie. We are looking forward to beginning your training. This is a very significant day for us all, as you have such a rare gift. However, there is a huge amount to learn. I will take you out into the forest for field work and Wolfe will teach you here about how to care for all our noble beasts."

Maggie gazed up into the greenest pair of eyes she had ever seen. Excitement started to fizz in her tummy and all she could seem to do was grin in response.

"Now, meet the twins," she continued, gesturing behind her.

Two tall teenagers loped towards her smiling. Both had dark hair with pearl highlights. The boy's was chin length and wavy and the girl's was a mass of curls tumbling down below her shoulders.

"I'm Elvi," said the girl, "this is Emil, my brother." Elvi linked arms with Maggie and Emil gave her a wave and a lopsided grin.

"First things first," Elvi continued, "let's get you some training gear to wear. Maggie looked down at her blue jeans and top and then glanced around at the others. They all wore a mixture of forest green tops and brown trousers, boots, belts, jackets, straps and pockets packed with goodness knows what. She followed Elvi, dying to see what the inside of the cabin was like.

The first room they came into was a lounge area with sofas, tables, desks and chairs scattered over the wooden floor. More animals and birds were asleep on rugs and cushions, or ambling contentedly around. Maggie's eyes were wide with delight and wonder as she took in the scene. Elvi laughed as she caught sight of her expression.

"You get used to it, I promise. We have so many lovely companions, some stay for a while and some stay for ever! This one is Hercules," she continued, scooping up a dear little field mouse from a tiny cushion on a windowsill. Hercules yawned, then ran nimbly up Elvi's sleeve, over her shoulder and dropped into her top pocket.

"Companions come in all shapes and sizes," she commented, "but tell me something, is it really true Maggie?" she suddenly asked, turning to face her, "is it true that you can talk to animals and understand them?"

"Well, it seems I have been able to with a few so far," Maggie replied, "it's all a bit new to me. I certainly couldn't before I came here. I can understand Storm and some turtles, a couple of eagles and actually, just now, Selene spoke to me too."

It was Elvi's turn to show wide eyed amazement.

"Wow, that's awesome! I wish I could do that!"

"Can't you?" queried Maggie, "I assumed we could

all do that in our School."

"No, there hasn't been anyone who can talk to noble beasts for, well, I don't know how long. We will have to ask Britta about that. She's in charge by the way. Wolfe is the lead Ancient for the School only because Britta doesn't want to go to the meetings. She is too busy out in the forest and in other realms, helping or rescuing noble beasts. She's the best, you will love her. And don't mind Emil, he's a bit of a practical joker but he is also really brilliant with all the beasts that live in water. As for me, the creatures I love most are land creatures. Britta is amazing with bird life and the more unusual creatures we come across from other realms."

By this time, they had left the lounge, continued down a dimly lit corridor and entered a changing room. Elvi opened a large wooden chest and rummaged through, pulling out garments of different sizes which she held up against Maggie. "Right, try these on for size and I'll meet you in the kitchen, just head straight through the other side of the lounge. Best to have a snack before Britta takes you out."

With that, Elvi turned on her heel and left Maggie to change her clothes. The leggings were similar to jodhpurs; dark brown and close fitting. The tunic was forest green with threads of yellow, lighter green and chestnut running through it. The boots were knee length; also a brown material but she couldn't tell what they were made from. They fastened up along the outside of her calves and felt light but sturdy. A sleeveless green jacket completed the outfit and Maggie slung on the tiny back pack which had been set out for her too. Good to go, she thought to herself. She smiled, thinking that she looked like a cross between Peter Pan and Robin Hood. Grinning again, she shook her head and decided to investigate a little bit further on her way back to the kitchen.

Maggie opened each door in turn as she retraced her footsteps. One door led into a lab of some sort with jars and bottles filled with herbs, salves, bandages and some interesting looking contraptions. What could they be for?

Another door led into a storage room piled high with equipment, rugs, feed and tools. A third door led into sleeping quarters with cosy looking beds with intricately carved, wooden screens dividing different areas. The final door led back into the lounge, so Maggie headed straight across to the opening on the far side, stopping to stroke the feathers of a frizzled, Polish hen, perched on the back of a sofa.

"Mmmmm, lovely," it murmured as she carried on by.

"Elder Fizzle or Damson Drinkit?" offered Elvi.

"I'll try the Damson Drinkit please." Maggie replied. She had tried the Elder Fizzle last time and it was delicious but she was keen to try out something new. It certainly didn't disappoint. Plum coloured liquid frothed and sparkled in her mouth. It was extremely thirst quenching too. A plateful of snacks lay on the table. Maggie recognised Mores, which were scrumptious biscuits, but she hadn't tasted the other ones which looked like flap jacks.

"Oat floats," explained Elvi as she noticed Maggie considering them, "totally amazing and packed with energy, they really do make you feel like you can float on air; great for long field trips."

After a few minutes munching, the girls went back outside to the porch to join the Ancients and Emil. "OK, Maggie," said Britta, "I think it's time to go out and start to get you familiar with the forest and begin to learn the pathways. We will check in on some of the noble beasts and find out what you can do so far."

"Oh, nothing really," replied Maggie, suddenly feeling a little anxious that she might let Britta down.

"Don't worry about a thing," reassured Britta with a twinkle in her eye, "just be yourself and see what happens. You may be surprised." With this Britta turned on her heel and strode out of the clearing. She obviously expected Maggie to follow. Maggie glanced over at Storm, but Storm was busy with Jedrek.

"You go," encouraged Wolfe, "Storm will be fine with us; she has a few things to learn too, Jed will keep an eye out for her. We will see you before lunch time."

There was nothing for it but to follow Britta and head out into the forest. She was both excited and a little apprehensive to see what the morning would bring.

James

James headed off with the other scholars towards the School of the Keepers of Knowledge. He felt very anxious, not knowing anyone or what would be expected of him, but he also felt intrigued. They approached a building, which he could identify as a library, though the entrance was not at all what he had expected.

James had researched many libraries in his spare time, as he was fascinated not only by facts and information, but how to store these. Some libraries, like the one he had visited in Dublin called Trinity

College, were dark and mysterious. It was two
stories high with wooden arches and he had seen
The Book of Kells; a highly decorated manuscript
which was over 800 years old. He had visited
several others on-line; a very modern, windowless
library, though surprising light and airy, was at Yale
University in America. One of the oldest ones was
The Tianyi Pavilion Library in China which was
built in 1560 and even displayed inscribed tortoise
shells! James really wanted to visit the Codrington
library of Oxford University in person. It was both
old and new with its traditional spiral staircases
and high tech reading areas. He had heard of eco-
friendly grass roofed libraries too, but he had not
had the chance to visit one yet.

A gently sloping mound led up and away from one
side of the forest. It was impossible to predict how
big this library would be, what style it would take
and how far below the earth it might go. James'
curiosity levels surged and he tiptoed forward to get
a good first glimpse of what lay ahead. Where was
the door? James watched closely as Madeleine, the

Ancient of their School, reached out her hand and rested it on the trunk of a gnarled tree, which arched so strongly it's branches touched the ground. You couldn't really say which end the roots would have come from, but it was clearly alive as he could see dainty white blossom speckling the branches. Suddenly, an arched portion of the green mound rose silently upwards, revealing a large circular platform with beautifully carved benches and framework around the sides. Madeleine ushered them on to the platform with an outstretched hand and the half dozen scholars tiptoed quietly forward. Clearly the others were as in awe as he was.

Little did James know that it would take him many months to explore the Earthlie's magnificent library. He had no idea at this stage that there were portals within the library which would take him to Japan, America, Australia and many places besides. But, he would never forget his first impression of this library. The platform moved slowly down to land silently below and the scholars walked out into an enormous circular area with a massive dome

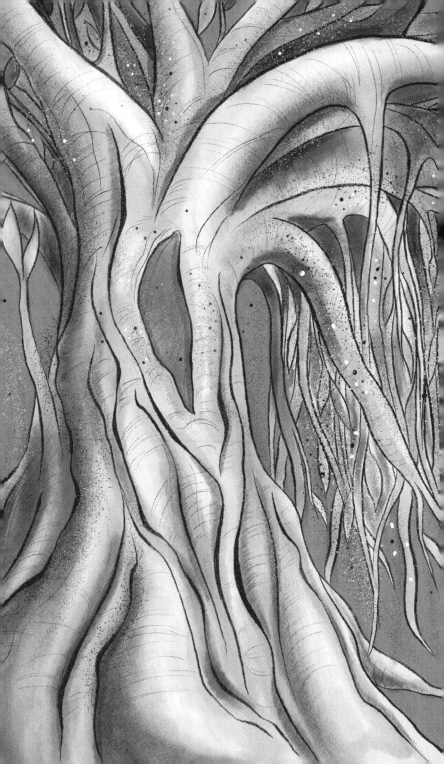

overhead. It was lit up by a fascinating, intricate skylight. Fanning out from a central courtyard were rows and rows of reading stations, like the spokes on a cart wheel. Many scholars were pouring over maps, books, manuscripts and inscribed artifacts. There was the quietest hush of murmured exchanges between the Scholars and the atmosphere was calm and orderly, putting James completely at ease. He knew he would love it here.

"You will all be assigned a mentor to show you around and help you find your feet," announced Madeleine breaking into James' thoughts. She was an older lady with a calm demeanour, beautiful blue eyes and pure white hair, streaked with their School's signature moonstone colour. Some of the scholar's streaks took on different hues depending on the light; pinks and grey hints were the most common.

"After your initial induction period, we will be able to decide which area you will be best suited to. We have several vast areas which span out from this reading room. Each area has a specialism; such as the Arts, Science, Music, Geometry, Language and many others. Some of you will provide invaluable service in cataloguing, some will care-take our collections and others will go out in to the field to research and collect new material. There are many more jobs besides, but you needn't worry, as we always find the one best suited to your unique talents and interests. I know you will be completely happy and will provide an invaluable service to us all and the library itself."

As soon as Madeleine had finished speaking, some older teenage scholars appeared at her side and Madeleine began pairing them up. James found himself beside a tall boy with extremely short ginger hair. He was very distinctive looking with cornflower blue eyes. He had a thoughtful, serious gaze but James felt comfortable with him at once, which was quite rare for him.

"I'm Melvil, but you can call me Mel. James, right?"

James nodded.

"Okay, let's begin the tour. It will seem like a never ending maze of rooms, walkways, spiral staircases and vaulted ceilings at first, but you soon get a feel for it all."

With that Mel headed off through one of the many arches leading out of the central reading room and James sped up to keep pace with his long strides. James glanced this way and that, taking in the many amazing sights, as Mel kept up a running commentary on what they were passing. He gave a brief account of certain collections and pointed out significant pieces of art and sculpture which dotted the walls and corridors they passed through. Finally they reached a cavernous room, which spiralled down and down rather than up and up. James peered over the edge of the balcony and his tummy flipped. Could he actually see the bottom?

"First things first," continued Mel, "this is our home area of the library but you can access almost anywhere else too. Some areas are restricted but I'll tell you more about that later on. The key thing to remember is that the different floors below can rearrange themselves according to what you are thinking about or what you need to find out about. We all have this talent. That means you don't necessarily have to travel to the furthest floors. I'm not quite sure how many there are to be truthful, more are being added all the time. There are also some really cool secret reading cocoons on some floors which I'll show you in due course. So, try it out, think of something you would like to find out about."

James immediately thought of three things at once; portals, cloaking devices and modern skylights. Mel chuckled, as with a quiet whir, the floors below began to seamlessly interchange.

"I can see we are going to get along." Mel said, still grinning at James' dumbstruck look, "why think of one thing when you can think of three! I have a little research of my own to do, so I will leave you to explore by yourself for a while and will come and find you before lunch. There is a lot to take in. Don't be alarmed if walkways appear or ladders slide close to you; the library is intuitive to your thoughts and will try to be helpful by bringing useful books and articles within reach. I'm on level 31 if you want me, just think about both me and the level and I will re-appear. I would start over there if I were you." Mel pointed to some stairs which led to a mezzanine floor above James' head. A comfy armchair could be seen beside an ornate wooden table with a reading lamp. A book was currently floating down from a high shelf to join the three already waiting for him. Without further ado, James headed towards the open spiral stairwell leading up to it.

Three hours later Mel appeared at James' side. "Come on, Book Worm," he teased, "I thought I had better come and find you instead, aren't you hungry?"

James' tummy rumbled to confirm that this was indeed the case. He remembered he had agreed to meet the other's for lunch, so quickly checked with Mel if this was allowed. Mel reassured him that this was quite alright and showed him a short cut from their part of the library to a lift which led directly

43

back to the central clearing. Amazing! You would never have known it was there. James pushed open a wooden door to find himself stepping out of an ancient Beech tree at one side of the clearing. He took a careful note of where it was and headed to the seating area to find his friends.

Lunch in the Glade

"James! Over here," called Maggie. She was pleased to see her friend arriving at last and waved him over to join her and the others. There was Quinn and Vita, Archer and some of the other new scholars. They were all lounging on curved, wooden deck chairs with soft cushions. Quinn and Vita's mum had sent enough food for them all to share and James was pleased to tuck in with the others. He _ had developed quite a fondness for Mores but he was brave enough to try out a few new tasty morsels too. Maggie was chatting away, clearly excited by the morning out with Britta.

"It was so awesome, first I met the only two other

scholars in my School, twins! Then I met some of the animal companions, they were amazing! After that, Britta took me out into the forest and she is starting to teach me how to track different noble beasts!"

James couldn't help but smile, her enthusiasm was infectious, if a bit tiring for him at times. He tried to explain about the incredible library but he could tell Maggie was not overly impressed that he had spent three hours just reading.

Archer and Vita sat together. Maggie and the others had helped to rescue both of them from The Wild Bandits in the Grimm's realm. Vita was training with Keithia, the leading Ancient of the Earthlie realm in the School of Nature and Nurture. She was learning about growing plants and travelling to different realms to bring back new species which could be useful to their community. Archer was about to commence an intensive training schedule with The Protectors. He was already quite skilful with the bow and arrow, but he chatted excitedly about all the different weapons and tools that were

now available to him.

Quinn sat down beside Maggie. "Doesn't sound like you are enjoying it much so far then?" he teased. Maggie grinned and asked him about his morning. He was in his second year at the School of Magic and Marvel. She had been intrigued by his skills on their first adventure out of the Realm and couldn't wait to see what he would be able to do next. Like Maggie, Quinn was an active character and they had got on well from the start. Both of them were natural leaders and had worked well together in their first rescue mission. Quinn outlined some of the skills he would be practising this year; how to cloak himself in order to work in stealth mode, how to summon objects he needed and, very excitingly, he was beginning to learn how to create portals. Very few could master this skill.

Lunchtime passed quickly and all the Scholars eagerly returned for their afternoon training sessions. The afternoon zoomed by and it seemed like no time at all until Maggie and James climbed the steps which led them home through the trap door. They both felt exhilarated by their first day at school and were already looking forward to the coming days ahead. Maggie was silent too, for once, as they strolled across the Green and made their way to their houses. She thought again how lucky they were to be experiencing magic right on their doorstep. Storm trotted beside her. She too was uncharacteristically quiet and looked like she was ready for a serious nap the second they got home. Storm had had an eventful day with Jedrek, beginning to learn how to support her companion and how to communicate with Maggie telepathically. Even if they were separated they would still be able to speak into each other's minds. Storm hoped there wouldn't be a need for this, as she already hated to be apart from Maggie, but you never knew what might happen in the Realms below and when these special skills might come in handy.

The days passed, one tumbling into the next, each one more fascinating than the one before. Maggie and James were leading double lives. One spent training and learning with their Scholar peers below The Green, the other doing the usual Summer holiday activities up above; swimming, day trips with their families, making dens and hanging out on The Green with Storm. They spent as much time as they could together, so that they could discuss everything about the Earthlie Realm. It was a happy time. A time of honing new skills, forging friendships and building up trust and unbreakable bonds. But, almost as if you can predict a change in the weather when the wind picks up, there was a sudden change in the atmosphere in the Earthlie Realm. Something strange and unsettling was happening in the forest, not something you could easily identify at first, but gradually they all became aware of something or someone lurking in the forest's shadows.

CHAPTER 5

Vince Asks for help

"We need to go out into the forest right now." Britta was waiting for Maggie, as she and James came through the Top Glimmer.

"James, you can carry on to the library," she continued, "Maggie, bring Storm."

Britta turned on her heel and strode off. Maggie and James exchanged worried looks before Maggie jogged quickly to catch up with her. Maggie glanced down and noticed that her normal clothes had already changed into her forest gear. It was just the same with their hair streaks. Passing through the portal seemed to activate or deactivate these things. Storm bounced alongside Maggie, thrilled at being asked to come too. She was growing into her huge paws and her shoulders reached just above Maggie's knees already. Storm too had been training with Jedrek each time they came to the Earthlie realm and she felt ready for action.

The forest was eerily quiet. Maggie realised the birds were silent, like just before an eclipse of the sun. It was spooky, you didn't realise how much ambient sound birdsong made, until it was gone. The sun still shone brightly as they passed through the main glade and headed deeper into the forest but the air of tranquillity and calm was no longer the same. It was very unsettling. Late Scholars hurried to class, worried frowns on their faces, everyone had picked up on the atmosphere and Keithia had called on Britta to make initial investigations.

"How long has it been like this?" asked Maggie, as their footsteps slowed into tracking mode. They crept forward stealthily, instinctively reading the ground and plants for clues.

"I could sense it yesterday evening. There was a strange feeling in the forest, but it was this morning when the birds did not sing their usual dawn chorus that I knew for sure something terrible must have happened amongst the noble beasts."

Maggie tried to reach out with her mind to detect animal activity. She might be able to ask for some help or check if any of the animals had seen anything. It was too still and quiet; the animals all seemed to be hiding from potential danger or attack. What could have caused this?

Finally, Britta stopped, holding her hand up for Maggie to follow suit.

"There," she indicated. Half hidden by a fallen tree lay a wounded pony. Maggie and Britta knelt down by the injured creature. Britta placed soothing hands over its coat checking for cuts or breaks. Brown eyes fluttered open and a weak whimpering sound came from the small pony's soft muzzle. Maggie listened intently.

"They've all gone through a portal! I don't know

where they are now. I couldn't keep up with them, my legs are too short. It was a trick though, I know it! Someone made a portal and lured the whole drift of ponies through. There was a trail of tasty hay and nuts. The portal closed with quite a blast and knocked this tree down too. I think my legs are trapped."

"Trapped, but not broken," Maggie reassured the distressed pony, "stay still and we will get you free. We will try not to hurt you."

Maggie and Britta worked quickly together to lever up the fallen bough enough to let the little pony wriggle out. Maggie translated to Britta what the pony had reported. Britta looked thoughtful.

"That's a problem," she finally said, "we have no way of knowing where the portal led. We would need strong magic to try and pick up its trail".

Maggie felt the pony nuzzling her neck and gave her a reassuring look.

"What's your name?" Maggie enquired, "How old are you?"

My name is Blessing and I'm nearly one. I was the last foal to be born this season. That's why I

couldn't keep up. My parent's will be so worried!"
"We will help you Blessing. We will get your family
and the rest of the Drift back." Maggie wanted to
reassure the tiny chestnut pony but she was feeling
very anxious inside. How on earth would they find
out where the Drift had gone and who had lured
them into a trap?

Just then, an almighty crashing sound could be
heard coming straight towards them. A creature was
blundering through the undergrowth, cracking twigs
underfoot and taking no care to be quiet at all. Britta
and Maggie both stood in a wary stance in front
of Blessing. Maggie could feel the foal trembling;
even her mane and tail were quivering.
"Good grief, if I had known it would be like this
I'm not sure I would have come at all!" complained
a familiar sounding voice.
"I mean first that chilly water and now this
ridiculously long journey. Honestly, are we ever
going to find them?"
Crashing out of the bushes in front of them, nearly
knocking them to the ground charged a handsome

but indignant looking alpaca.

"Vince!" exclaimed Maggie.

"Maggie!" Vince exclaimed back, digging his hooves into the soil and coming to an ungainly halt. "At last, I can't believe it! We've found you! Honestly, I had no idea it would be so difficult. First we came through the portal you left through. There was water, salt water! I mean really! We are land animals, Imari and me. It was shocking, I can tell you, and our fur got completely soaked! Then we had no clue where to go and two gigantic eagles came swooping out of nowhere towards us. I was terrified, I can't deny it! Poor Imari thought they were going to snatch his daughter from under our very noses! As it turns out they were rather helpful, they showed us the way to this forest. I'm very grateful actually. Quite hungry though, it has to be said."

Vince stopped for breath and Maggie couldn't help but grin. This dear, funny, Alpaca had been such a help to them on their first trip to the Grimm's Realm and bizarrely not only could he talk, but everyone could understand him, not just her. Maggie took in the sight of Imari; a beautiful Vervet monkey, holding on to Vince's back. Sitting in front of him was his little girl, Amara. When Maggie had last said goodbye to Vince he had been on his way to help reunite them. This followed their escape from Argatron with the help of Vince and the entire Snug of Alpacas. Maggie shivered at the memories of Argatron, the capital city in the Grimm's realm, where she, James and Quinn had travelled to in order to rescue Vita and Archer. They had encountered many frightening Grimms and The Wild Bandits. Shaking her head to get rid of the dark thoughts, Maggie quickly updated Britta and Blessing as to who her friends were.

"Let me help you there Mags," interrupted Vince, "the reason I made this infernal journey, was to get you to come back and help. That dastardly Snatcher chap has turned his attention to Noble Beasts now, as well as still trying to grab any Implings that he can. A whole Drift of gorgeous little ponies has been corralled through a portal into The Dark Wild and he is planning to hide them until the next market day in Argatron. They are so sweet, I really

couldn't bear it.

I just knew you were the girl to help, and your friends too of course. That is why I have risked my very hooves to come to this rather wonderful Realm." Vince glanced around as if he had only just noticed what a majestic forest it was. Imari added his voice,

"You will come, won't you? We really need your help."

"Britta?" queried Maggie, "we can go, can't we?"

"Absolutely," confirmed Britta, "I will need to get Blessing back to our cabin and have Wolfe look after her. Storm, run ahead and meet Jedrek. Tell Jed everything and he will alert Wolfe. Then you need to gather up a team. There's no time to lose."

Storm felt immensely proud that she had been given such an important mission and so, with a quick lick to Maggie's hand, she headed back the way they had come.

"You go ahead with your friends," ordered Britta, "I will bring Blessing; it will take us longer with her bruised legs."

Blessing blinked her beautiful eyes and struggled to

her feet beside Britta.

"Lead the way, Mags" said Vince. "There is room for you too, climb aboard."

Maggie sprung up on to Vince's broad back and immediately recalled how beautifully soft his fur was; as soft as velvet. Vince sprang forward in his usual exuberant manner and the three riders clung on for dear life. This would be a quick journey back.

Maggie grilled Vince for any details he could remember about the capture of the Drift. Her mind was whirring as she made quick decisions about the team she would need as there was not a moment to lose.

CHAPTER 6

Back Through the Portal

By the time Maggie was leaping to the ground in front of the cabin she had decided who her team would be. No surprise that she had chosen Quinn, James, Vita and Archer but she wondered if she could also ask Selene to accompany her. Storm of course would be coming too and she reasoned that she could call for back up if needs be. To her surprise Selene was already pawing the ground and looking intently at her.

"I'm ready."

Storm had done a brilliant job of updating Jedrek who had conveyed the information telepathically to

Wolfe. Wolfe in turn had sent word to the other Scholars who would be there shortly and he was waiting to welcome Blessing to see what he could do to make her more comfortable and to treat her injuries. Elvi and Emil stood to one side looking serious.

"Those poor darling ponies," murmured Elvi, "I can't believe I didn't know, I feel terrible, I've let the Drift down."

Emil tried to reassure his sister. "Listen Vi, there is dark magic at work in the forest, you heard what has happened, no one can know what the Snatcher will do next. Maggie will find them and we will be ready as soon as she sends word."

"And time to do something about the Snatcher too!" Quinn had appeared in the clearing and had a thunderous look on his face, "Enough is enough. The Snatcher has a powerful magic ring which enables him to conjure portals. I've been hearing rumours about it in School. We need to get that ring back before anyone else gets captured."

"One step at a time Quinn, but yes, we need to take action," Maggie agreed, "where are the others? We need to get going."

Just as she spoke James, Vita and Archer tumbled into the glade and there were several moments of blurred activity as Maggie briefed the team, the twins gathered packs, clothes, food and equipment for them and Wolfe offered words of advice. Storm trotted around Selene's mighty hooves while Vince and the Vervet monkeys explored their surroundings.

"Right, let's go!" rallied Maggie, "Selene says she will take me, Quinn and James. Vince can you take Vita and Archer?"

"Of course! These shoulders are as strong as an ox!" He winked at the pair he had been sent to rescue in the Grimm's Realm.

"We can travel through the forest canopy,"
announced Imari with Amara nodding beside him,
"you just watch us go!"

They all assembled, an unusual but determined
group of children and animals, setting off back
the way Vince had come. Just as they came to the
edge of the clearing they saw that Britta, guiding
Blessing, had arrived safely. Wolfe rushed over
to support the little pony as she limped into view.
Maggie was spurred on even further to rescue the
Drift of ponies and reunite Blessing with her family.

Vince led the way, feeling rather important and it
wasn't long before Maggie caught sight of the two
sea eagles whirling above the canopy. Pontus and
Thalassus had befriended Maggie in the past and
even let her and the others travel on their mighty
wings.

Maggie found she could direct her thoughts to all
of the animals in her company; an amazing skill she
had been practising over the past weeks. She was

able to reassure the monkeys that the eagles would not harm them and relay to Vince, Storm and Selene that the eagles would continue to be their guides back to the portal at Turtle Bay. Selene immediately leapt forward, overtaking Vince and began galloping at an adrenaline inducing speed, weaving through the forest trees. Maggie grinned, not only did she love travelling fast but she caught a miffed expression on Vince's face as they whizzed past him which was very comical.

"Go Vince, go!" she encouraged. Maggie knew that he could run incredibly fast too and, sure enough, within a few moments all the children were hanging on for dear life; the wind blowing their hair back and their faces stinging with the sensation.

In the end the journey didn't take as long as Maggie feared and just as the sun was dipping low in the sky the party tumbled out of the thinning forest and onto the high cliffs overlooking the beach. The sea eagles soared over the edge and with mighty thrusts of their wings swooped down to the sea to catch some fish. Selene moved a lot slower now as she picked her way down the rockier incline leading to the beach. Maggie knew exactly where the portal was this time and they all made their way along the golden sand toward the caves. As luck would have it, the tide was out and they were able to get across the rippling sand to the fourth cave, barely getting any hooves wet. Maggie was a little worried about the trip through the underwater passageway which would lead to the hidden cave with the portal. How on earth would the animals manage?

She needn't have worried however as magic is of course called magic for a reason. Maggie waved at the turtles as they passed by one another in the cave entrance; no doubt off to find some more pretty shells to take to the secret cave. She let Quinn lead the way and to everyone's amazement, as he slipped beneath the water, the tunnel began to widen and the children all gasped. One by one, with a little splashing and grumbling on Vince's part, the team ducked below the water and held their breath as they swam quickly along the passage way. Each one gulping in big mouthfuls of air the second they broke through the surface on the other side. Once again they found themselves standing amongst beautiful shells in a wonderful cave with the magnificent shimmering portal.

The children re-mounted their trusty steeds and, with Storm and the monkeys in between them, they stepped forward into the glimmering portal.

Where is the Drift?

The journey through the portal seemed to move in slow motion, but the second they hit the ground in the Grimm's Realm, both Selene and Vince surged forward strongly. Vince took the lead again, as this was his territory and they headed East through the rough, rocky moorland.

James was not unhappy to be part of this rescue mission but he was always a little anxious at the best of times, and he couldn't help but think longingly of his beautiful library back in the Earthlie Realm. He was really getting to know his way around the different levels and was forming great friendships with Melvil and Madeleine; he admired them both enormously. He also thought he would be a lot more comfortable back in a cosy reading nook immersed in research. What did he know about ponies? Strangely enough, he reflected, quite a lot. His mind dredged up a few facts and figures as he flew through the air behind Maggie. He knew there were about 16 native breeds, from the tiny little Shetland pony to the giant Clydesdale in Scotland as well as several moorland varieties too. Part of him worried that he might not be much use to the team on this trip but then again he had played an important role last time in getting the group out of Argatron, away from the Grimm ogres, and all whilst being pursued by The Wild Bandits. Time would tell.

They got further and further from the portal and James was beginning to wonder if they would stop for a rest soon. It had been a long time since breakfast and his tummy was rumbling furiously. Just as he thought he might have to call out to Maggie, Vince came to a screeching halt using his hooves as anchors. At that exact moment a Glimmer caught their eye and to their horror they spotted a familiar sinister figure disappearing through just as the Glimmer snapped shut.

"What? What!" he shouted indignantly, "Where? Where! They've gone! They were right here when I left, I don't understand it!"

Sure enough they all gazed into an empty, make shift paddock that had been hastily erected by The Snatcher in this far flung, wild moorland in the east of the Realm. There was not a single pony to be seen.

"He must have moved them, but where?" continued Vince, "oh, why didn't I set a guard? Why did I rush off without thinking?"

Vince was looking very forlorn. His kind heart and best of intentions were often thwarted by his impulsive nature; he looked absolutely devastated that the ponies had been whisked away again to

goodness knows where.

James suddenly had an idea. "Hiding in plain sight," he stated.

"What do you mean James?" Maggie asked.

"It means that if you hide things where they are visible then they will be unnoticeable."

They all stared at James still not quite understanding what he meant.

"If you wanted to hide a book you would put it in a library."

"Oh!" exclaimed Maggie, starting to grasp his meaning, "that is so clever! But wait, how on earth are we supposed to know where you could hide a whole Drift of ponies without anyone suspecting?"

"Well that's just a simple process of elimination. The mountain and moorland ponies, or M&Ms as they are sometimes known, fall into distinct groups. We just need to search through them until we find the Drift. Colouring would be a distinguishing feature too and a good place to start."

They all gazed at James. Maggie was so proud of her friend. He really was a walking fact file; their very own search engine.

"There are a few pony species in Ireland like the Kerry bog or Connemara ponies, or in Scotland there are Galloway and Shetland ponies, and in Wales they have Welsh Mountain ponies and not to mention several varieties in England. There are the Dales, the Fells, the Dartmoor, the Exmoor and the New Forest ponies to name just a few."

Maggie's face fell. Not only was it quite an extensive list but there was also the not insignificant problem of travelling to these places. If they had to go all the way back through the portal at Turtle Bay, travel back to the Earthlie forest, up through the top Glimmer to reach The Green, they would still be at square one. Then what? But James hadn't finished yet.

"The size, temperament and distinguishing features of the Earthlie forest ponies would help to eliminate some of these species."

"Plus," added Quinn, "I don't think the Snatcher could manage to get a whole Drift of ponies through a portal to anywhere other than the near Upland. It would take powerful magic to achieve that, and whilst he uses the ring, that is his only source of power. He has no real magic of his own."

Maggie pondered this information and offered up the facts she had learnt about the ponies so far.

"Well, they are different colours but mostly bay or chestnut and they all have brown eyes. They are super friendly and really enjoy delicious grass along with a nibble of gorse sometimes."

James considered the facts. Sadly, Maggie's

description could still apply to a few moorland breeds but did seem to rule out a couple of varieties too. After a few moments reflection, he offered his opinion.

"The New Forest," he stated. "It would be the closest place in England for the Snatcher to get to. It is a National Park with heath and pasture. It covers quite a large area from Hampshire into Wiltshire and towards Dorset. The ponies wander quite freely and have right of way, even on roads. It would be the perfect place to hide the Earthlie forest ponies until market day arrives."

"Right then, let's go!" shouted Vince, whirling around, "no time to lose!"

"Wait, Vince," Maggie cautioned her impulsive friend, "there is the small matter of how we get there. Any chance you could rustle up a portal, Quinn?"

Quinn and the Portal

Quinn had already been thinking about the logistics of the operation whilst James and Maggie were talking. It was true that part of his training this year had included conjuring up a portal. He hadn't shared the fact that this was not at all usual for a second year Scholar in the School of Magic and Marvel. In fact it was virtually unheard of for anyone to train in conjuring portals, or Glimmers, as he thought of them. It could take years to perfect the skill. Quinn, however, had showed early promise and his Ancient had singled him out for extra one to one lessons. He could actually open a portal in practise sessions now, but he had never

79

had to hold it open long enough for groups of people to go through, never mind a Drift of ponies. Plus, he wasn't completely sure he could create a Glimmer that would take them to exactly where they needed to go. He did agree though that valuable time would be wasted heading all the way back to the trapdoor Glimmer, the one portal that did lead to the Upland, as even then they would still have to travel undetected to the New Forest.

Quinn was always the sort of boy to face a challenge head on and so, with no time to lose, he stepped forward.

"Yes, perhaps I can conjure a Glimmer. I mean, I have." Vita and Archer gasped. These two knew the rarity and powerful magic needed for this possibility. Vita was immensely proud of her brother and all eyes were now glued to Quinn.

"I can only try my best. I will need to focus hard. Should it work then let's all be ready to go through as quickly as we can as I don't know how long the

Glimmer will stay open."

The others all nodded and stood to one side as Quinn raised his hands, closing his eyes as a fierce look of concentration came over his face. Several tense moments went by, beads of sweat appeared on Quinn's forehead and the other children were beginning to feel quite anxious. Vince, Selene and Storm, however, stood poised for flight. They sensed that every second would count and were determined to be ready the second the Glimmer opened.

Suddenly, and dramatically, Quinn threw his arms wide with an almighty yell and there before their very eyes was an actual Glimmer, shimmering just above the ground. Then, just as suddenly, it abruptly closed and Quinn sank to the ground looking thoroughly down hearted.

"Try again, Quinn," Vita encourage her brother, "keep trying, you can do it, I know you can."

They all nodded and tried to support him as best they could. Quinn rose to his feet again, concentration etched once more on his face. This time as he flung his arms wide there was a dazzling flash as a strong and tall Glimmer opened right in front of them. Incredible! The children and animals surged forward, Selene ducking her head as she galloped through. Quinn was the last to go and as he lowered his hands the Glimmer shrank so rapidly that he had to throw himself forward and dive through the closing gap.

"You did it Quinn!" praised Maggie, "that was unbelievably awesome!"

Quinn got to his feet looking a little dusty and weary but very proud of his achievement. His friends' eyes were shining at him and James held out a handful of Mores to help him recover. Quinn just hoped he would be able to get them all back too, as well as the ponies. For now though, he glanced around, as did Maggie and the others. It was important to quickly get the lie of the land.

"I've never been in Upland before." Quinn uttered, suddenly struck by the enormity of what they were doing. Vita and Archer too were gazing around a little awe struck.

Quinn wasn't finished with surprising his friends. He saw that they were in a quiet area of the forest, there was grass underfoot and the trees were thinning out ahead. He reasoned that they were not far from a clearing or Uplander dwellings and so he wanted to make sure they would be safe and could travel undetected.

"Gather round," he instructed, "first we need to disappear from sight. I would imagine that the local Uplanders have not seen many alpacas with a group of children out by themselves, and they definitely won't be familiar with a goigil. I'm going to manipulate an area immediately surrounding us to camouflage us. It will work a bit like a bubble but it will move with us. If you stray too far from it you will become exposed, so we must stick close together at all times."

The children mounted their trusty steeds and Storm sidled up close beside Selene's legs. Again Quinn concentrated intensely and, with a sequence of complex hand signals, he created a marvellous cloaking bubble. It was quite difficult to see. It appeared to be a shimmering dome which fitted quite neatly over and around them. You could just detect the edge of the dome in the breeze, as it rippled in the air current. Quinn explained that they while they would easily be able to see out, animals and humans would not easily detect them, unless they had magic powers of their own. Maggie thought this highly unlikely, but then again, her life had changed beyond recognition, so you couldn't discount the possibility of there being pockets of magic elsewhere.

"Right then, James," Quinn startled James out of his thoughts, he had been lost in contemplation mulling over what he had just experienced, "time for you to take the lead again, my friend. Just say the word and we will follow."

James nodded once and pointed toward the thinning tree line. The intrepid group, in their camouflaged dome, headed off again with great determination in their hearts to continue their rescue mission.

CHAPTER 9

Battle to Rescue the Drift

Was it a trap? Maggie wondered, as the makeshift paddock came into view more quickly than she had anticipated. It almost seemed too easy to have found the Drift so soon, but then again, the Snatcher hadn't had a lot of time to plan things out carefully.

Searching the area as they approached, Maggie signalled for them all to slow their speed and exercise caution. The Drift seemed to sense their as yet unseen approach and they were skittish. A few snorted and whinnied, drawing more attention. All of the group were feeling nervous, as if waiting for impending disaster to strike. And it did!

From nowhere and with an almighty battle cry The
Wild Bandits stormed out of the undergrowth on the
East side of the paddock, sling shots in hand and
war in their eyes! Vita, Archer and Maggie gasped
collectively and were momentarily paralysed.
This was not something they had foreseen. How
had they made it through the Glimmer? Shaking
herself abruptly, Maggie signalled for them to
rapidly skirt the paddock to the West. She darted
a glance at Archer indicating for him to launch a
defence. Almost instantly Selene reared, roaring in
an appalling manner. The Snatcher had appeared
right in the middle of their escape route. His arms
were held aloft with the legendary Enchanted
Ring sparkling in the sunlight. Selene veered west.
Archer dropped to the ground drawing his bow
seamlessly. He launched an arc of arrows to shield
the escaping team. Not just ordinary arrows, but
magical cluster arrows. They spread out in a wide
arc and exploded into dazzling sparks, accompanied
by a dense fog which confused The Wild Bandit's
advance. Curses and stumbling could be heard as
they clumsily shot stones from their slings which,

none the less, only just narrowly missed their targets. Vita had risen to her feet like an acrobat, balancing herself nimbly on Vince's back, raising her hands and concentrating on her own skills as intensely as she could. She drew plant material from her surroundings and formed a flexible lasso which she whirled above the ponies.

Maggie and Selene rode like the wind, kicking up dust, straight towards the paddock. With a splintering crack, Selene kicked the nearest wooden struts hard and they instantly crumbled. Turning, she galloped directly at The Snatcher who was desperately muttering an incantation to open a new Glimmer to stage another escape. Archer kept up a relentless defence, throwing enchanted hand grenades which released irritating scratchnitch bugs. These hornet like creatures honed in on their targets, stinging and biting anything in their path. They dissolved after 12 seconds but the nauseating stench they left behind was truly horrific. His favourite weapon he saved until last; the Quaker.

Archer quickly surveyed the battle front. His heart surged as he saw Vita's lasso. Even as he turned back he could see her whirling and twirling the vine into an ever larger circle over the heads of the escaping ponies. The instant Selene had broken the first paddock struts, the Drift had emerged, like a hungry swarm of bees, pouring through their exit as one continuous group, desperate to get away from the battle. Vita had to make sure her lasso encircled every last pony so that they could be herded back towards the protective bubble. It was a sight to behold.

Archer glimpsed Selene's advance on The Snatcher and his heart momentarily quelled, as he feared the incantation would be completed before Maggie could stop him. Could he still take the Drift and Maggie too? With no further time to hesitate, Archer drew the Quaker from inside his jerkin. It looked like a mega blaster, but was deadly silent on activation. As he pressed the trigger, time seemed to come to an immediate halt; The Wild Bandits were caught in mid-air and mid shot, Selene and Maggie

froze as they reared at the Snatcher and Vita's lasso hovered above the entire Drift who were momentarily stilled, with manes and tails streaming and hooves kicked high. For an agonising minute there was complete silence; the chaotic scene was almost peaceful. Then, with an almost visible shudder, everything sped up and pandemonium broke out.

The Quaker had caused a mini localised earth tremor which threw the Wild Bandits to the ground, dazing them instantly. Vita's lasso fell exactly into place and she and Vince charged straight back towards the direction of the dome. Selene and Maggie almost collided with the Snatcher, but with a sickening feeling, Maggie gasped in dread. As if in slow motion, he finished his incantation, threw out his hand with the Glimmer ring and cast open a portal to his right. Unable to stop what was unfolding before her very eyes, she could only watch in horror as the Snatcher sneered straight in her face and took a simple side step through to another Realm. In an instant the Glimmer snapped

shut and Selene landed right where he had been.
Maggie's anger and frustration coursed through
Selene and she swept around in equal exasperation.
She wanted to protect the escaping Drift from
the rear. In fact there was little danger now, as
the Wild Bandits had fallen into retreat and Vita,
still balanced on Vince, was fast approaching the
direction of where the dome should be. Archer was
running at full speed to catch up with the Drift.
Selene galloped alongside him while Maggie leaned
down to extend an arm out for him to catch onto.
Maggie swung him up behind her and with the
ever faithful Storm right by her side they charged
forward to catch up with the others.

A tremble in the atmosphere, a ripple in the current,
a shimmer in the air and there was James, leaning
out of the dome and waving frantically at them.
With signals, he directed them in to a thinner, longer
formation and one by one, the ponies disappeared
from sight, straight into the dome and on through
the new Glimmer which Quinn had simultaneously
opened. Maggie tried to calm the ponies as they all

made this transition. She hardly had time to wonder where on earth or indeed under the earth, they would end up this time, before she felt Selene gathering her strength and jumping into the rippling dome.

CHAPTER 10

Where Are We?

It was complete an utter chaos for several minutes with ponies careering around and the team all talking at once. There were questions and confusions on all sides. Where were they? Had they made it to safety? Was everyone ok? How had The Bandits got there and were they still stuck in the New Forest?

First things first though, Maggie used her calming communication skills to settle the Drift and assure them they were out of danger, for now at least. Maggie and James knew exactly where they were but were at a loss to explain how they had ended up there. They were right in the middle of their very own Green in their very own village. Perhaps because Quinn had heard them talk about it and knew that the Glimmer the Uplanders travelled through to the Earthlie Realm was in the form of a trapdoor on this very Green.

"Quinn!" urged Maggie, "can you cloak us before the whole village sees us? This is our home, a whole Drift of ponies have never just materialised out of thin air before on the village Green. There is bound to be a fuss!"

Quinn shook his head, he was exhausted. He had used more magic in this rescue mission than he had ever used before in his entire life and it had taken its toll. Nonetheless, he knew how important it was to avoid suspicion. There was no easy way to explain why they had dozens of ponies gathered on the village Green. Concentrating with his last reserves of energy Quinn threw his arms wide with an anguished cry. The dome appeared! He fanned it wider still until it encompassed every last grazing pony and finally slumped to his knees, hands to the ground. How long it would hold, he couldn't say.

James was looking rather amazed and bemused by his familiar surroundings while Archer and Vita had thrown themselves to the grass in a tired heap. Vince could be heard boasting to Selene who was gazing at him in a very cool manner, rolling her eyes occasionally.

"Yes indeed, I led the rescue back to safety. I took control, gathered every single one of those darling ponies and got them securely back under the dome and straight through the next Glimmer. Audacious and brave you might say, but not me. No trouble at all. No need to thank me, a pleasure, an absolute pleasure to be of service. Feeling a little hungry now as it happens. To be expected I suppose with all the energy I expended in the daring dash. Think I'll just have a little nibble of grass and perhaps catch up on my beauty sleep for a few minutes."

Now what wondered Maggie? She could hardly invite everyone home for tea and she really wasn't sure that the ponies, never mind Selene, would fit through the trapdoor. Quinn seemed utterly spent and she felt quite anxious for him. It would be a while before he would be able to attempt another Glimmer.

'Snack?' suggested James and actually, Maggie thought, it would be just the thing to top up their energy levels while they considered what options lay before them. Explaining to the others that they would be back in a few moments with a little picnic; Maggie, James and Storm slipped out of the dome and raced home to gather supplies.

'Meet you back here, James!' Maggie called out. Within 10 minutes they had arrived back, both with a bulging back pack of provisions. It was the Earthlie's turn to look surprised at the Uplander's offerings and to sample their snacks. There were Wotsits and Jammmy Dodgers supplied by James along with cartons of orange juice. There were cheese and marmite sandwiches hastily put together by Maggie. She had also brought apples, tomatoes, grapes, Chocolate Fingers and a bagful of dog biscuits for Storm. Nothing could be heard except crunching and munching for quite a while and then, when everyone was completely full, they stretched flat out on the grass.

"How do we get home?" Archer queried, voicing the question at the forefront of everybody's minds.

CHAPTER 11

The Journey Home

It was no problem heaving up the trap door and sending Vita, Archer and James straight back to the Earthlie Realm. James planned to head directly to the library to do some much needed research on the Snatcher and the enchanted ring he possessed. Vita and Archer would debrief Keithia, as head of the Realm, and Maggie also sent Storm, who proudly charged ahead of the children to alert Brita and Wolfe of their imminent arrival.

"You can rely on me! I'll let you know when I get there; do try your best to listen out for me." Storm called back. Maggie shook her head; she sometimes

107

wondered who had the most confidence, Vince or Storm?

Quinn stayed with Maggie doing his best to keep the dome over the Drift. Meanwhile, something was weighing on Maggie's mind, as she scanned the ponies looking for one particular pair. There they were. A pair of beautiful ponies, restlessly pawing the ground, unable to settle and graze with the others; ears flat and tails twitching rapidly. They must be Blessing's parents; they looked so forlorn and anxious. Maggie headed straight over to them and gazed in a friendly manner straight into their eyes. Quinn watched but he could only imagine what the conversation might be; a snort and a few whinnies, some more urgent swishing of tails, followed by an excited neigh and then finally they looked much calmer. Their tails relaxed and their ears pointed forward. There was nothing to be heard on Maggie's side. He was secretly impressed at how far her communication skills had come in such a short time.

"Good job, Maggie," he congratulated her as she returned.

"Ah, they are so sweet and so thankful that Blessing is safe with Wolfe. They can't wait to see her, so I tried to assure them that we have a plan and it won't be long before they are happily reunited."

Quinn raised his eyebrows at this last comment.

"I know, I know, give me a minute, I'm working on it."

Just then, as if foreshadowing impending disaster, the wind lifted, the branches of the stately trees swayed and the leaves rustled briskly. Maggie could immediately sense a slight tremble in the atmosphere and knew that magic was afoot again. To her absolute horror and not 20 metres away from where they were cloaked, there appeared a tear in the atmosphere. A Glimmer had been created and out stepped the Snatcher! How? Had he been able to follow their Glimmer? Did they leave a trail?

"Quinn!" whispered Maggie urgently. "Look! We've got to keep the Drift safe. We need to think fast!"

Quinn's expression changed to one of fierce concentration and then to shock. Following the Snatcher out of the Glimmer came the Wild Bandits! Were they working together now? Maggie focused her skills on keeping the Drift calm; a few had spotted the Snatcher and tails were starting to twitch. Maggie concentrated; she didn't want to give the Snatcher any clues as to where the dome was. Surely he would be able to detect them? The Bandits had started to prowl around the Green making jabs with their hands and sticks to test for cloaking devices. Maggie could feel her heart rate speed up and adrenaline surged through her.

"Quinn!" she whispered again, " I know you are exhausted but is there any way you can widen the trapdoor Glimmer rather than create a new one, if it is just a bit wider and taller we could get the ponies, Vince and Selene through safely?"

Quinn nodded, indicating that he would try. Selene was on full alert, ready to protect Maggie at any cost. Vince was snoring gently, hooves twitching, re-living his heroic rescue no doubt. Selene poked him in the side with a hoof and glared at him coldly.

"What's that, what's that? Yes, absolutely awake, ready for action as needed. Good grief! How did that nasty fellow get here? Are those the bandits too? I just can't believe it, I take a moment out and you let everything go to pot!'"

He aimed this last comment at Selene and swiftly shuffled behind her as if to say: this is your mess, you deal with it.

For a long tense moment it seemed as if time stood still, then, once again, everything erupted into action and absolute chaos ensued.

CHAPTER 12

Battle on the Green

The sheer effort it took for Quinn to focus on widening the trapdoor Glimmer meant that his concentration momentarily lapsed on keeping the cloaking dome intact. The bubble disappeared for several crucial seconds and that was all the time it took for the Bandits and the Snatcher to hone in on them. The Snatcher snarled and lifted his hands wide. Maggie could see his lips moving again, it was only a matter of moments before he opened another Glimmer. It was clear that the Bandits were working with him, as they immediately leapt into action; cracking whips and hollering war cries as they started to round up the panicking ponies. The

Drift was completely spooked; some ponies bolted, others shied away, tension could be seen in the set of their mouths. Their ears were flattened and the whole field was filled with an agitated swishing of tales and frantic whinnies. Maggie looked on aghast; her skills were not fully developed, there was no way she could bring such pandemonium under control in the few moments she had before they were whisked away from right under her nose. She risked a glance at Quinn and saw concentration etched on his face.

Maggie's head was buzzing with the sheer enormity of the situation. What should she do?

Just as she was beginning to despair that, not only would she lose the Drift when they were so close to home, but also that the whole village would arrive to watch the spectacle, she heard Storm's voice loud and clear in her head:

"Storm here, reporting in! Don't fret, back up is on its way, we'll be there soon!"

Seconds later the trapdoor flew open and out came Keithia, Britta, Storm and Zephyr: the Ancient from the School of Magic and Marvel. There was a blur of movement as everyone swung into action.

"Couldn't let you two have all the fun now, could we?" Zephyr grinned at them both briefly clapping Quinn on the back before turning his attention to the Snatcher.

"Draw the ponies towards the Glimmer, Maggie," ordered Britta as she swept her gaze over the Drift searching for injuries.

The Wild Bandits screeched with horror at the sight of the Ancients, but the Snatcher stood firm, chanting faster and faster. Keithia was a sight to behold. As the senior Ancient of the School of Nature and Nurture she was able to manipulate many things around her. With flashes of her hand, new vines shot from neighbouring trees, grabbing and twirling the Bandits one by one until they were tied up tight in the highest branches, unable to move

so much as a little finger. She created tiny tornadoes to confuse and herd escaping Bandits back towards her so that not a single one escaped. Maggie concentrated all her powers on enticing the Drift directly towards the trapdoor. Despite the commotion, Maggie had an extremely soothing effect on their nerves and in small groups the ponies' direction shifted, as if drawn by a magnet, closer and closer to the Glimmer.

Zephyr targeted the Snatcher. With fury flashing in his eyes like firecrackers, he strode purposefully toward the Snatcher, arms wide and incantations flowing from his lips. With an almighty crack which echoed across the whole Green, he slashed the air with his right hand, opening a Glimmer instantly. With his left, he levitated the Snatcher and slammed him straight through the tear and into the beyond. With a thunderous clap of his palms, the Glimmer snapped shut and the Snatcher was gone. Zephyr glanced around and observed his pupil with pride; Quinn had mustered his remaining energy to widen the trapdoor Glimmer. Maggie, Selene, Vince and

Storm led the way with Britta close on their heels; the Drift was pouring down the steps back to the Earthlie Realm. Keithia nodded at Zephyr, indicating he needed to deal with the Bandits before they were done and then turned and strode gracefully toward the Glimmer herself. The entire skirmish was over within minutes, but Maggie felt sure she would be reliving it in her dreams for several weeks to come.

The ponies surged out into the clearing and headed off with a flick of their carefree tails to all corners of their precious forest. All except for Blessing's parents who followed Maggie and Storm anxiously back towards the cabin where Wolfe was waiting with their darling filly foal. It was the sweetest of reunions and Vince welled up as the ponies nuzzled one another.

"I do so love a happy ending." Vince sniffed. "Honestly, we alpacas are as hard as nails, but now and then it's good to let it out, don't you think?"

Maggie grinned and gave him a hug whilst Selene looked on scornfully.

"Vince, my friend," she said, "you are as soppy and as soft as your fur and I wouldn't have you any other way."

A muffled harrumph could be heard but Vince hugged Maggie back, finishing off with a slurpy lick right across her forehead.

"Vince! Enough with the licking!"

Maggie didn't really mind. She dropped a gentle kiss on Selene's muzzle as she headed in to grab a shower, mumbling to Brita that she would fill her in on all the details later. It was a good job the Ancients had stepped in when they did. They all had a lot to learn still Maggie reflected stepping over Storm, who had crashed out on the porch. She thought that she might have to have a quick snooze herself before she met up with the others in the clearing for a planning session. They had a lot to discuss and she was especially keen to get her training underway again. Maggie knew all too well, that wherever Zephyr had banished the Snatcher and the Wild Bandits to, they would be back before long.

CHAPTER 13

How to Catch the Snatcher?

Later that day, the scholars met in the clearing, refreshed and still feeling on a high from their successful rescue mission. There was a hubbub of chatter for some time as they relived moments and shared details with each other. Maggie felt so proud of all her friends; they were a great team and she couldn't have hoped for more. Her face clouded over however, as she began to think about the task ahead. There was much to learn and a lot of preparation to be done before they could hope to set out to catch the Snatcher.

"So," Maggie broke into the chatter, "we have

carried out a very accomplished rescue and we rightly need to celebrate that. Before we do though, let's just spend a few moments sharing ideas on what we all know will be our greatest mission ever; catching the Snatcher. We can't always be on the back foot; following his lead and solving the problems he creates. We need to take charge and lure him into a trap. James, any news on the ring? That seems to be the key."

James looked up, a little startled at being singled out to give his advice but, as it happened, he had spent most of the intervening time with Madeleine, the Ancient of the School of the Keepers of Knowledge, and his mentor Melvil. They had been scouring books in the library and Mel and Madeleine had shared everything they knew with him about the ring. So he could, in fact, share his knowledge.

"The ring is incredibly old and belonged to the original Ancient of the Realm, long, long before Keithia's time. It's a complicated story but for now, the simple version is that many years ago there was a battle between the Grimm's Realm and the Earthlie Realm. The Grimms somehow managed to band themselves together with horrible creatures and came through a Glimmer created by one of our own scholars to attack. The Scholar was from the School of Magic and Marvel, a boy called Brocwulf. He had grown jealous of his Ancient's skills and angry that the Ancients would not let him use the Enchanted Ring to create Glimmers of his own. He got a team around him from different schools and carried out an audacious plan to steal the ring and open the Glimmer for the Grimms. He had high hopes of becoming something like a King in the Grimms Realm. It didn't quite go to plan however, even though he got the ring. The Grimms were too brutish to pay him any homage or loyalty in their Realm and he became isolated, forever banished from his own Realm. The ring does not grant immortality but it does slow his ageing. Unbelievable as it seems, the Snatcher is Brocwulf. He got his nickname from the Implings over the years who have been rightly terrified of him. Madeleine thinks he has another wicked plan up his

sleeve as his mischief making and snatchings have become more and more prevalent in recent weeks."

Several moments of silence followed as they all digested this long speech from James and considered the impact of the information. Quinn, Vita and Archer hadn't known the full picture and the group's serious faces reflected everyone's sombre mood.

"Right," Maggie interrupted their thoughts, "can I suggest that we all meet here at first break tomorrow once we have had time to sleep on this new information and bring our ideas to share? We mustn't rush our plan or underestimate the power the Snatcher has. However, time is of the essence and we need to act soon, before he carries out another Snatching, or worse."

The others all nodded in agreement.

"For now, though," Quinn announced, "there is some celebrating to be done! A certain alpaca has already begun on our evening picnic."

They all glanced over to the spread which had been laid out by scholars from all the different Schools. Vince looked up as he felt the weight of their gazes and grinned, crumbs spilling out of his mouth.

"These Oat Floats are amazing!" he called out, spitting crumbs everywhere, "we alpacas have to keep up our strength, you know. These missions take up a lot of energy. Muscle power. Brain food. You lot could probably do with a little nibble too, I should think."

An amused snort came from the tree line and Selene appeared, striding majestically towards Vince. There was, however, a little twinkle in her eye as she nudged Vince out of the way for the children to come and eat their fill.

Dusk fell, candles were lit and the lilting tunes of a violin and a bodhran, a traditional Irish drum, could be heard, as Scholars and Ancients filled the clearing to join in the celebration of the ponies' safe return to the Realm. For now, thoughts of future action were put to one side as everyone enjoyed the moment.

CHAPTER 14

Home Again

It was quite some time later before Maggie and James lifted the trapdoor and walked back out on to the Green. Maggie gazed around in disbelief. Not a blade of grass was out of place, you would never have known what had happened just a few hours earlier. Zephyr had done a fantastic clear up job.

"Bye James," Maggie called, giving a half wave in his direction, as they both headed home.

James just nodded, deep in thought. Storm was surprisingly quiet, ambling along beside Maggie's knees.

129

They went in the side door which lead into the kitchen and Maggie fed Storm straight away. Storm practically inhaled her meal and headed straight to the lounge to collapse on her bed. Almost before her head hit the cushion muffled snores could be heard. Maggie smiled and turned to give her mum a cuddle as she stirred something on the cooker.

"Hello, hunny pie," her mum greeted her giving her a one armed hug, "nice afternoon with James?"

"Yes. We were hanging out with Storm. Is Hamish home?" Hamish was her step dad, an amiable Scotsman.

"Yes, he has gone to his study to watch the cricket and relax for a bit. I think he's been working too hard. Do you know, he tried to tell me there was some sort of circus on the Green earlier? An odd chap in a pointed hat and some ladies in strange costumes with some sort of pony act. Well, I ask you. What's that all about? I looked out of the kitchen window when he called me but didn't see a thing. He must have been pulling my leg, though he seemed quite serious."

"Ha ha, he probably was mum. A late April Fools maybe. I wouldn't worry; the cricket will do the trick."

Maggie headed into the lounge, turned on the tv and followed Storm's example by collapsing on to the sofa. Her eyes were looking at the screen but her mind was miles away and her brain was whirring. After a while, a little smile turned up the corner of her lips. She had an idea which just might work…

Book 3 - Battle for the Enchanted Ring

The adventure continues from where it left off in Book 2.

An exciting third adventure full of our favourite characters and dramatic action. The Lammas Challenge is set for the end of August. All Scholars may enter but just one will win the opportunity to wear the Alpha ring. It is hoped the Fair will lure the Snatcher to the Earthlie Realm in an attempt to steal this powerful ring too. The Scholars and The Ancients work together to bring about a dazzling three day fair full or music, entertainment, trade and good food. But who will win the Lammas Challenge on the last day, and have the Scholars taken on too much in a third clash with The Snatcher?

134

Battle for the Enchanted Ring reviews

REVIEW **- Oscar age 8.**

REVIEW - **Griff age 10**

Keep reading for a secret peek at book 3...

135

CHAPTER 1

How to Catch the Snatcher

Maggie dashed down the stairs into the Earthlie Realm with Storm close on her heels. She had called an emergency meeting in the clearing during their first break but had something to do first. Quinn, James, Vita and Archer were waiting as she and Storm arrived a little late.

"Sorry," Maggie apologised for her delay, "there was a bit of a squabble between neighbouring sets of badgers so I had to go and help them sort it out. It was a territory dispute but thankfully all is resolved now."

The others smiled at Maggie. They were almost used to her unique skill of talking to animals

137

but they still found it rather amazing and very endearing.

As usual Maggie took the lead. With no time to waste, after their recent adventure, she got straight to the point and asked everyone to share their knowledge of the Snatcher so that they could pool their thoughts on how to catch him and retrieve the Enchanted Ring before he struck again. She turned to James first and asked him to recap what he had found out at the School of the Keepers of Knowledge, with the help of Madeleine, the Ancient Scholar and chief librarian, and his mentor Melvil. James looked a little embarrassed at being in the limelight, he would much rather blend into the background. However, he briefly outlined what he had gleaned.

"There was a battle between the Grimm's Realm and the Earthlie Realm in a bygone era. The Grimms banded themselves together with predatory creatures and came through a Glimmer, created by one of our own scholars, in order to attack. The Scholar was from the School of Magic and

Manipulation, a boy called Brocwulf. You will remember that the Snatcher is in fact Brocwulf. He had grown jealous of his Ancient's skills and was angry that he was not permitted to use the Enchanted Ring to create Glimmers of his own. He gathered a wayward team around him from different schools and carried out a bold plan to steal the ring and open the Glimmer for the Grimms to come through. He had high hopes of becoming a King in the Grimms Realm. It didn't quite go according to plan however, even though he got the ring. The Grimms turned on him and he was banished forever from his own Realm."

This was virtually the same account that James had given before and the others nodded to indicate they recalled these facts. Quinn stood next and relayed what he had learnt from his Ancient in the School of Magic and Marvel.

"Zephyr tells me that the Enchanted Ring is one of two archaic jewels worn by the original Ancients, Elsha and Alden. They were so powerful that few were trained to wear and use them, and as time went by, they were no longer worn but instead fiercely guarded. One was guarded by the School of Magic and Marvel with powerful charms and spells. These were thought to be unbreakable. The other ring was kept safe by the School of Nature and Nurture; I believe Keithia is the current guardian of this ring."

"How did Brocwulf manage to get the ring?"

Maggie asked the question on everyone's minds.

"Actually, the full account is not known," continued James, "what we do know may not be entirely accurate either. The records might be part truth and part legend. It is written that Brocwulf had 'bad blood' and the Scholars in the School of Magic and Manipulation found him strange and unfriendly and left him to his own devices. He became isolated, and whilst he studied hard, there was neither guidance nor explanation of how to use his skills for good. He delved deeper and deeper into dark magic from books that were considered to

be cursed and banned from use. Who knows
how far he drifted but it does seem that he was
eventually tainted with evil. It is recorded that he
colluded with the Grimms, who as we know are
far from intelligent. What they lack in brains they
more than make up for in brawn. They were to
be the army behind him and he thought he would
be able to rule over them, but he was ultimately
outnumbered. As for the theft itself, it is described
in slightly fanciful and mystical language. It seems
he learnt a powerful and dark incantation, which
cast an immobilising spell on the original Ancient,
Alden, and then he somehow broke the charms set
to guard the Enchanted Ring. From there, he used
the magical skills he had acquired to conjure the
first Glimmer. His reward was immunity in the
Grimm's Realm; he may not be harmed by anyone
or anything. As we know, he became known as
The Snatcher due to his evil habit of kidnapping
Implings and taking them to be enslaved by the
Grimms."

Silence followed this detailed explanation from

James, who looked flushed from his uncharacteristically lengthy speech. Archer, who studied with The Protectors, led by the Ancient Liath, spoke next:

"An additional challenge will be to disarm the weapons and trickery he now uses. As we learnt on our last quest to free the Drift, he has allied the Wild Bandits. We know how wily and fierce they can be; trading anything they can capture in the Grimm's Realm. His magic spells have become steadily more powerful over the many decades since he stole The Enchanted Ring. We cannot afford to underestimate his skills."

"However," added Vita, who studied with Keithia at the School of Nature and Nurture, "he has no real affinity with the natural elements; earth, water, fire and air. He can only try to manipulate these but without a true connection to the elements he will never have full control. We have the upper hand there. Also, there are five of us and we are getting stronger all the time."

Quinn smiled at his younger sister. She had a peaceful soul and loved harmony and goodness but she had the heart of a warrior when her Realm was threatened. She had more than proved her abilities in the last quest.

Maggie's mind was buzzing, she already had a few thoughts about how to trap the Snatcher and all of the information shared had helped to shape it.

"OK," she announced, "I've had an idea but it is a bit dangerous and we would need to act quickly."

BELOW THE GREEN

Recipe for Oat Floats

Makes 12 or so.

Ingredients:

150g butter,

150g light brown soft sugar,

4 tbsp honey,

300g porridge oats,

100g frozen raspberries,

edible shimmer.

Method

1. Heat oven to 200C/180C fan/gas 6

2. Line a 20 x 20cm baking tin with parchment.

3. Melt the butter, sugar, honey and a pinch of salt in a pan. Once the mixture is bubbling and combined, stir in the oats.

4. Tip the oat mixture into the lined baking tin and press down with your fingers or the back of a spoon. Scatter over the raspberries, then lightly press them into the oat mixture.

5. Bake for 25-30 mins until golden brown. Leave to cool, sprinkle on some shimmer and then cut into 9 or 12 flapjacks.

Dear Reader,

Thank you for continuing with the adventure, I know you will love book 3 which is my favourite so far! If you haven't already done so, have a listen to a clip of the audio book either on my website arhetherington.com or on Amazon. The amazing voice artist, Karen Ascoe, has narrated the first book beautifully and really brought my gorgeous characters to life. I can't decide which is my favourite now, Vince or Imari, or is it Storm?! Let me know your favourite character and what you would like to know about them.

I hope you have been on the website to download the recipes for free, Mores from book 1 along with Elder Fizzle and the Oat Floats from book 2; fun to make and so delicious to eat! I have just finished the first draft of book 4 which might even take over from book 3 as being my favourite; there is an epic under the sea adventure and battle. I am now researching book 5 and can't wait to get going on that one.

See you in the next book!

Annelise R Hetherington

Printed in Poland
by Amazon Fulfillment
Poland Sp. z o.o., Wrocław

62631317R00089